A Gift For: Mommy & Daddy

Love
From: Binjamin

For Jerry and Nancy, my parents

Copyright © 2010 by Marla Frazee.
Published in 2011 by Hallmark Gift Books,
a division of Hallmark Cards, Inc.,
under license from Beach Lane Books,
an Imprint of Simon & Schuster Children's Publishing Division

BOK1169
ISBN: 978-1-59530-389-9

Printed and bound in China
JUL11

starring

the Boss BABY

AS HIMSELF!

by **Marla Frazee**

BEACH LANE BOOKS   New York   London   Toronto   Sydney

Hallmark
GIFT BOOKS

From the moment the baby arrived,

it was obvious that he was the boss.

He put Mom and Dad on a round-the-clock schedule, with no time off.

And then he set up his office right smack-dab in the middle of the house.

He made demands.
Many, many demands.

And he was quite
particular.

If things
weren't done
to his immediate
satisfaction,

he had a fit.

He conducted meetings.

Lots

and lots

and *lots* of meetings,

many in the middle of the night.

The funky thing was, he never, ever said
a single word that made any sense at all.

But that didn't stop him.

As boss, he was entitled to plenty of perks.

There was the lounge.

The spa.

And the executive gym.

There were drinks
made to order,
24/7.

And, of course,
the private jet.

Then one day, all activity ground to a halt.
The boss surveyed his surroundings,
eyeballed his workers, and frowned.

He called a meeting.
His staff did not respond.

He called and called and called. Nothing.

The boss's usual demands were not getting their usual results.

It was time to try something
completely out of the box.

Ma-ma? Da-da?

Wow. That worked.

For the first time since his arrival,
the boss baby was pleased.

But only momentarily.

He had to get back to the office ASAP.

There was still a business to run here.

And make no mistake . . .

he was the boss of it.

If you have enjoyed this book,
and have a boss baby of your own,
we would love to hear from you.

Please send your comments to:
Hallmark Book Feedback
P.O. Box 419034
Mail Drop 215
Kansas City, MO 64141

Or e-mail us at:
booknotes@hallmark.com